2112

Written by

NEIL PEART

Screen Play
Written by

DARIN GRAVES

2112
Copyright © 2022 by Darin Graves

ISBN
978-1-958122-44-0 (Paperback)
978-1-958122-43-3 (eBook)

Table of Contents

PROLOGUE

I believe that Neil Peart true message of 2112 is art or his definition of art concluded by the multitude or individual. The diversive range of the products of human activities involving the conscious use of creative imagination, to paper or product, to express technical proficiency of ideas, beauty and conceptual methods. Neil Peart has written lyrics for the band Rush that are beyond price.

The interpretation of 2112 is that there is a leviathan of galactic war, societies or sodalities mean a specific group who increase power by taking over entire planets, yes, that does happen in 2112, but Neal's verifiable and accurate idea is that the individual rights is declined by the society in control. The planet that is appropriated or taken over by The Priests of the Temples of Syrinx, kill the leaders before them but keep the masses in order. Their music, their paintings, their sculptures, their drawings and all types of art are controlled by the "great computers", within their hallowed halls. No individual art is allowed, by punishing the people or person who broke the Priests law. Their only art is from the Priests. The pictures and paintings and all art, especially music, is given by the priests and controlled by the priests, any alterations by the masses or an individual is punishable by law.

Within this interpretation of "2112", a planet is taken over by the military power of the Priests of the Temple of Syrinx, over the planet, the Priests watch in their spacecraft hovering over the planet while their military comes out of hyper space, hundreds of them, attacking the planet and taking out defense systems, destroying space ships and city structures, laying waste to them and making room, expansing space for the new order, the Temples of Syrinx.

During the attack, 3 men are seen speaking to each other, 2 of them are leaders amoung the existing planet, have been figureheads and principals for dozens of years, the third man is in a suit for space travel, cannot see his head, after their transmission and conveying knowledge and ideas he gets into a spacecraft, quickly joins another 50 ships above the planet's surface. All 50 of these ships go into hyper space, going away from the war which is taking their planet over. The Priests see this in their craft and tell their own troopers to let them go, we want the planet, let the cowards run. The other 2 men stay, realizing that the masses of the planet will still need leaders, but they realize that there is a new order, new captains who control the planet, the Priests of the Temples of Syrinx......

As the movie opens it is forwarded by a series of Rush more favorable songs. It will probably have Geddy Lee Bass commercials as well as Alex Lifesons guitar commercials as well. Both will have Rush songs doing most presence in the minutes to half hour it takes.A succession of songs that will show Rush pictures from the 1970s to now, it will finally end at the back cover of 2112 showing the main classic photo!

First

Chapter

Showing the 2112 back cover photo Of Rush, slowly fades to show deep space, 10,000 stars can be seen. Slowly the camera fades going down to a blue and green planet. Blueprinted much like Earth, it contains 5 billion people. The mass of people are controlled and under scrutiny by Megadon, it is the primary city and structure which controls the political and direction for the planet, he who controls Megadon controls the supervision and administration of the planet. The Priests realize this city will ultimately lead to the control of the planet. A massive ship comes out of hyper space above the planet, the Priests of the Temples of Syrinx. Seconds later smaller attack crafts, a dozen at first, then hundreds attack Megadon. Within the larger space craft, the figurehead, the master, flicks his wrist, and colossal missiles fire from their ship and take out defense systems at the speed of sound. The Priests watch as their military turn admirable and elegant buildings and structures into ash. The men, the individuals in control of the planet now try everything to defend their beloved planet, 500 of their attack ships were annihilated before they could get off the ground by quick missiles that fell like lightening bolts, 90 percent of the structures and architectures were burning to cinders. On the ship where the Priests were watching the take over of an entire planet, the Priests Overlord had instructions to his general who was military leading the attack:

PRIEST

"General, I want the debris and ash of the old Republic removed immediately, have the Guild clean this rubble and put our new Edifice and structures into tact now. Collect the leaders of old representative government, do not eliminate them all, let the ones we need to rule the masses, the people live. We will have some respect from the masses if we allow them to keep some figureheads and leaders." The priest looked at the generals eyes, made sure he had his attention.

"Commander, you know exactly what the Priests of the Temples of Syrinx demands. The total and direct control of this planet. We discovered thousands of years ago that the diseption of true control goes through the individual, not the collective. If I control a group, a small percentage will fade away and start a rebel, but I start from the individual, and move to the next, all will be easily controlled, it takes time, but it is a clearer way to control. The Art of this state, the craft of paintings, novels, writings, drawings, poems, modernism, the visual characteristics of lines, colors, values, shapes, textures, plays and movement will be punishable by law."

GENERAL

"Yes...of course Priest, it will be taken care of."

PRIEST

"The new field of order...will be our way of art. The most considerable art is music. Within our structures and buildings our computers will be the electronic brain for all art. Our hallowed halls will fill the ears of the masses. Any art will be given to the masses by our computers. The Temples of Syrinx are apart or the Solar Federation, our new structures of Megadon City will light up the stars! I want the Red Star of the Solar Ferderation to be seen from space."

GENERAL

"As you wish, my lord."

A couple miles south of the rubbles of Megadon City, at an airport stood 3 people, the flames and fires of the city could be felt, explosions of the dying city could still be heard. Gabriel has been a community leader for years, his best friend, Andrew were communicating with Nigel. Gabriel and Andrew watched as Nigel got into a smaller space craft and went into the atmosphere above them, along with 50 smaller crafts. They coordinated their sytems and went into hyper space. The priests in their enormous space station saw the crafts leaving.

PRIEST

"Let them go...cowards. We want the planet...the people of Megadon... What use have they for you?"

Second *Chapter*

20 days later, the old Republic is removed, the Priests in control under the Solar Federation have built new structures, amazing constuction. The Baltan Sea is the water supply for Megadon City, it is 850 miles long but its width is only 5 miles across where Megadon is located. A massive edifice is placed on either side of the sea, facing each other across the water, each are 6 miles high with bridges built across Baltan, it has an east and west but it is still called Megadon city. Toward their top, the massive structures have Opaque Art Projectors, they will be luminating a red Solar Federation Star 8 miles across, perfect sphere with a pentagon star inside it. All red, it can be seen 500 miles away and can be seen in space. The star illume during tha day and bright light at night. The control of the Projectors is a large floating office, floating in the water between the towers.

Grace to Glory was the name of small floating city in between the structures on the Baltan Sea, it floats in the water perfectly between the shores of the buildings that hold the Opaque projectors, it has control of any projections the edifice will give, through computer chips. A ceremony was taking place on the top deck of Grace of Glory, there were 20 Priests with 50 military guards to protect. There were 30 leaders and teachers of the old Republic, a small percentage of the ones that were not eliminated.

The ceremony could be seen threw the entire planet, threw camera, it delivers waves to every station of every city.

PRIEST

"Megadon City and all cities of this beautiful planet, the old Republic no longer exists, we the Priests of the Temples of Syrinx, through the Solar Federation are in control. This is a great day! Your lives will be finer, healthier, greater and superior than what it was before. From we the priests, we belive you are cured!"

Gabriel and Andrew looked at each other but never said a word, they were well aware of the Temples of Syrinx, they will make sure all of the masses will do it there way. Cured is a strange way to say "taken Hostage".

PRIEST

"The Priests have been around for thousands of years, we are quiet of conscious, calm in our right, confident our way is best. From generation to generation we, through experience know what will rule and control. Economically you shall be wealthier, threw our eyes of the systems and closer galaxies through trade and economic status we will summit and pinnacle other planets, compared to other planets we will peak and exceed. People, relish and enjoy!"

The people clapped, the new order savored it, leaders of the old order clapped to save their lives.

PRIEST

"Our new order of art is now in place. The computers within our hallowed halls will fill your intesity and passion for music, plays, drawings, paintings, conducting, sculptures and any group activity. Our music will be listened to, yours will be forgotten."

"The 2 new structures and edifices we have designed, there is an Opaque Projector on both of them that will emit a scene in the air well above us, we will put up a rainbow of the Solar Federation....a star! David..."

DAVID

A man in a peach pale color robe went forth, "Hello people, putting this physical scene together was hard yet easy. I hope you enjoy." He pointed to a man standing by the control panel and put a chip inside the machine and hit the enter button. Instantly, the Red Star of Solar Federstion went skyward, it filtered the air to let only red come out of the light, structured the shape and light, red in a circle with a pentagon in the middle. It was filtered through the air, you could walk right through it and feel nothing. It was 8 miles across. Everyone clapped as the new order, Priests of the Solar Federation marked their control of the planet. While clapping Gabriel and Andrew looked at each other.

THIRD

Chapter

6 months later:

Gabriel and Andrew had been leaders on this planet for years, when Nigel hyper spaced with many other ships when the Priests attacked, he went to a different arm of the Andromeda where friends lived in a contrasting divergent Solar System. Gabriel and Andrew kept looking to the stars, waiting for a sign of his return....

Gabriel and Andrew were scientists, quantom mechanics was there hobby, they would travel to different parts of the planet to seek artifacts from the past, to learn of different socities and there ways. David was younger but very enthused individual, he joined them on there trips to learn of this planets past. There travelling machine was a jet parcel, it flew above the ground at your choice at up to 300 miles an hour, so far away places were easily found. It could hover at ground level so it was a very good choice for their endevor.

GABRIEL

"Are you guys ready?" Andrew gave a thumb up.

DAVID

"I am looking so forward for this, follow you Gabriel."

Their jets went about 500 feet above the ground and acclerated to over 250 miles an hour, well above trees and various buildings. They were following the Baltan Sea shoreline toward the south, many small sites could be found in that area. Their jets are 12 feet long, can easily take tools with you when you need to dig in or filter soil around any finds you make. From the speed of the jets they arrived at their first site within an hour. Their jets hovered above an open grass land about a mile from Baltan shore line.

ANDREW

"We have been in this area before Dave, but we always find something new."

GABRIEL

"We are walking south and going towards those trees", pointing towards the south. "Why don't you head toward the shore line, there are pillars of rocks and caves near Baltan shore, I have been there once or twice before, its pleasurable if nothing else. You never can tell what you find."

ANDREW

"We are about a mile from the shore, take your equipment with you, it is gorgeous down there, if you don't find anything you can take lots of pictures."

DAVID

"Sounds good, and guys, thank you for taking me with you, just need to get away from things every once in a while." The Star of the Solar Federation could still be seen from your jet. David went down towards the Baltan shore, as he got closer there were more trees and shrub in the way. When he came through the tree line there was a silver and grey sand for 30 feet before the waves of the water hit sand. Bewitching and captivating view as you could see the twin moons even through bright sun light.

"Amazing....could I find a fitter more superior planet than this?", he whispered. He sat in sand and observed the gorgeous scenery. He thought to himself, where is this galaxy could I find a better view. He used his cell to take pictures, it could hold 50k if need be. Used his binoculars and could see rocks and cliffs toward the north, best place to look. 20 minutes later, the escarpment was stunning, the bluff lead to caves, some small and some big. Gabriel and Andrew would know what to look for, all I can do is enjoy the look. He came down from a solid rock area which lead into a medium cavern which he discovered a rock circular fire scolding, ancient, used many years ago. Light started to fade as he got deeper in the cave, "Fascinating", he whispered. He saw something...eaned against larger stones, still enough light to see..."What......", it was a straight neck. He came closer, he could see what it was...an instrument, from the past. He was looking down at a guitar, covered in dust and grime, he remembered as a child how he played one once. He did not know what to do, take pictures...grab it? He quickly thought of Gabriel and Andrew, he never touched it or took photos, he left the cave, got back to the jets and they were both there.

ANDREW

"So what do you think, find anything or just enjoy the perspective, the outlook is a beautiful panorama".

DAVID

"Found nothing, simply enjoyed the area." As Gabriel and Andrew were climbing on their jets, David looked back, he was intoxicated, drunken with desire of the instrument. He thought, "Will be coming back here soon."

Fourth Chapter

Several days went by, David was enhanced, gloated by the "guitar" he saw in the cave by Baltan Sea. He was looking forward to joining Gabriel and Andrew on their hobby to glimpse at and percieve the planets past. He picked up his cell...

DAVID

"Hello"

GABRIEL

"Hi Dave, ready to explore some different areas, Andrew and I know of a place up northeast that have several old and forgotten cities and communities, always find something relevant there".

DAVID

"I was hoping we could go back to the sea shore, where we were at last time".

GABRIEL

"Why....did you see something...you need to take another look...did something enhance
you".

DAVID

He was not used to lying, but could not help it, "No...I just enjoyed the view, the look and scenery there was amazing, would just like to go out there again".

GABRIEL

"Ok, I will call Andrew we will go back there again, there is some material, some textile substance we need to see again as well".

DAVID

"Alright, tomorrow morning?"

GABRIEL

"Same place and time, later".

David was excited, he did not know what he was going to do, maybe the guitar will be gone, who knows? There were several scripts, films and books he kept hidden, the Priests of the Temples of Syrinx were wary, cautious and circumspect about any and all art being under their control, punishable by law. He looked over his scripts concerning older musical instruments, must be hidden well when I am done reading, he had heard the Priests were sending out agents to destroy the older arts, they were making sure their art was the only one existed. The next morning was a beautiful day, the structures that held the illuminating Red Star of Solar Federation was shining with reflected light. Each edifice was 6 miles high and held whole cities within it's frame. The star itself was 8 miles across and shined day or night. David career was fulfilling the Opaques with power and strength to hold the Star for a thousand years if the Priests had it their way. Months have crossed since the Priests took over, all people on this planet were happy yet sad, economically the planet gained 10 fold in income but the Priests did exactly what they said, the only art and aptitude and talent will be done by them, no one else, listen to theirs only. The morning dew raised across the plains, the building the Priests put in were gorgeous, all people lived in future sky scrapers, everyone was happy...but

GABRIEL

"Good morning, David".

DAVID

"Hello, Andy, Gab, are we ready?"

ANDREW

"Yes...David, why do you want to go to the same place again, there is one big planet waiting to be seen?"

DAVID

"I just enjoyed it so much, the caves and rocks and water just had me aware of true beauty, I just feel like seeing it again".

ANDREW

"Ok, let's go".
They started their jets, spurt very quickly to hundreds of feet high and to 220 miles per hour. It took very short time to get back to the Baltan shorline, good speed from their jets. They all landed on the same hill they were before.

GABRIEL

"Like I said before Dave, Andy and I know where some artifacts are located, we will be seeing you ina little bit, have fun."

DAVID

"Sounds good, I just remember some spots with excellent views, I will be taking lots of pictures."

ANDREW

"Enjoy."

It took very little time for David to find the cave where the guitar was at. Following the Baltan shore line, the caves were in between tree lines and hundreds of bushes and sea weeds. He slowly entered the cave, his mind was excited by the instrument but he also knew the danger of the Priest and their alternative of ideas done their way or no way at all. Several yards in he saw it, even with light disappearing. He stopped, and looked at its head and neck, thought, "This is the most adorable and alluring instrument I have ever seen. I belive I can still play it..." He walked right up to it and stared, "Beautiful." He picked it up, swept off debris and dust, "It needs to be tuned, hopefully the strings won't break". He walked toward the caves enterence, sat on a rock formation and started playing. He tuned it himself and was lucky, strings never broke. He played chords, a pleasing combination of unanimity. Getting all the strings in circumferance. Playing certain strings and chords which he remembered, playing some songs he recalled. He was pleased at the sound it made, the concept was even in his ears. Resonation almost seemed perfect. He smiled, loved how it sounds, some harder chords he hit. About 25 or 30 feet away were Gabriel and Andrew, watching and listening, David was unaware of their presence, smiling happily as he played, loving the moment. Gabriel and Andrew were smiling as well, audience of a one man show. David played for a good time, the back of his mind, the Priests, against what they belived in, but how could they say this instrument could somehow be against them? This consonance, this euphony, this attractive pleasing sound should belong to everyone, should it not? He brought a zipper bag with him, put the guitar in it. When he got back to the jets Gabriel and Andrew were already on their jets, both looking at David, not saying anything but had questions in their eyes. They looked at David for several seconds.

ANDREW

"Hey David, did you enjoy the trip, did you find something...what have you got in that bag?" David could no look at either of them, he put the bag on the side of his jet. He thought of the Priests and their thoughts of individual art will be allowed only by themselves. He thought there has to be another way. Could I show the Priests the freedom of individual art? The sound of this instrument is stunning, the freedom it gives you as you play it.

DAVID

"I.....found something exraordinary...an instrument...it plays so beautifully."

GABRIEL

"Can we see it?"

DAVID

"Yes... of course...you have open minds...unlike the Priests." He pulled the guitar out of the bag, even sitting in the grudgy dusty dark, it looked magnifiecent. It was very rare, of a history, to play the guitar, natural and relaxing as one learns the chords and strings. He leaned on his jet and started playing. Gabriel and Andrew smiled and looked at each other. David remembered songs he played before and they came back to him instantly. They listened for several minutes, Dave had talent.

GABRIEL

"David, the Solar Federation controls most, not all of closer systems. They have put the Priests of the Temples of Syrinx in control of ours.

They can be ruthless if things do not go their way. Andrew and I have had jurisdiction and authority of this system for dozens of years, before the Priests. Life is so…beautiful and pleasing, if the system is run, with what you said before, open minds."

ANDREW

"We are the very few the Priests let live, David. The Priests want to dominate not just systems and planets, but people. In their own way they stand above us. They despise the way we ran our planet. Like they said, everyone on this planet is doing well financially but individual freedoms have been taken away."

GABRIEL

"The guitar you are holding now goes against how they control you. They are not worried about the instrument, what they are worried about is your freedom as you play it, the guitar means nothing, your individual freedom does, they need that away from you to control you, put you in order."

ANDREW

"What are you going to do with your guitar, the Priests think of it as nothing but a gadget, another toy that killed the ancient race of man."

DAVID

"I can't help it, this is what I was thinking, they should not hate something they know nothing of, when they see the prospect, the fine implementing tool, it could open their hearts and minds, I think they would like it more than you know." Gabriel and Andrew looked at each other. Several thoughts went through their minds. "Could you guys talk to the Priests, give me an audience through them, show how important this could be to the individual." Gabriel and Andrew both looked toward the sky, knew David's idea was precisely what should be done.

GABRIEL

"David, we could talk to them, it is easy for me and Andrew to read their minds. We know of their philosophy, their doctrine and ideology. That is what what we are saying right now, you should think of what wants you to be a friend but is actually your enemy. They would be an audience for you simply because you have to keep your enemies closer than your friends. Yes, they would be your audience, but I don't think you will like what they would do to you and your instrument."

DAVID

"There is a portion of my mind, my heart and soul who thinks you are wrong, I see this intrument, love how it feels, love what it does to me. I think the Priests will see that too!" Andrew and Gabriel looked at each other, neither one wanted to say no to David, Nigel will be bringing allies, forces to bear! The Priests of the Temples of Syrinx will leave or be annihilated, their choice.

GABRIEL

"We will make sure the Priests will be your audience."

FIFTH

Chapter

On the bottom of the stuctures on the west side, the Priests had a massive chamber right beneath their business subdepartment. Their computers along the halls were capable of holding massive amounts of information. Priests in brown robes were corroborating and validating the entire control of the planet, power, water, structure control, business transactions, food despencers, legislative branch of government, any and all that flows through Megadon must first go between around or within the Priests computers. The computers control everything, all actions where the people do business is monitored by their computers. There is very little that can be hid. The music and art are restricted and the technique and aptitude of enjoyment must go be allowed threw the Priests, the people are entertained only if the Priests allow it!

Gabriel and Andrew were given the jobs of keeping in contact with the Priests for any and all substandard or inferior procedures what the individuals or populates were engaging in. They spoke to the Priests, David was given one quarter of an hour. The Priests never sat, 15 of them, including executives and higher standard ones were there.

GABRIEL

"His name is David, he requires your audience, your attention to a musical instrument he found at the shore of the Baltan Sea, it was hidden in a small cave. From his history he has some knowledge of how to play this instrument." Gabriel looked at Andrew for a second, "David feels that the Priests will find it within their hearts to see what imagination and vision one can find within this instrument, this beauty."
The Priests stood still, no movement as they watched David pull the guitar out of his bag and sat down to play. He was in the middle of the chamber, played several notes. He played an entire mystic rythms as he played several more songs. The Priests never budged, other individuals of mankind listening to him play seriously enjoyed his work, his labor, before the Priests arrived they would have applauded, yet stood still. David played one more song to the Priests, the high order Priest stepped forward, stopped, looked down at David, still sitting in his chair.

PRIEST

"Your name is David?"

DAVID

"Yes."

PRIEST

"And you know how to play this.... toy?"

DAVID

"From when I was young."

PRIEST

"I see..." The Priest took a step forward, looked at David with thin shimmering eyes. Grabbed the guitar from David violently and smashed it like an axe on the floor, again and again. David looked at Andrew and Gabriel, mouth and eyes wide open. The guitar was wrecked and ruined as pieces of wood went flying across the floor. The look on the Priest face was anger and annoyance, an irritated vex! Screaming out loud at David, "Do you have a home?"

DAVID

Stood and looked at the Priest, bewildered and confusion, "Yes...."

PRIEST

"Give me the keys!" David had a look of confusion, he was hoping they would love or at least look into this instrument, what it would mean to people. He looked at Andrew and Gabriel, brought out the plastic card, his key to his home. The Priest grabbed it, "Does anyone else lived there?"

DAVID

"Just me." The Priest folded and broke the key.

PRIEST

"Guard, find out where this man lives, empty his furnishing, all movables and fittings, all fixtures and have them burned." David looked like he was already convicted, he wanted the guitar to open their minds on individual freedoms! He could see threw their actions he failed. Andrew and Gabriel were right. "Put in a new system and put it up for sale!" The Priest looked at David, "What is your employment?"

DAVID

"I…work for the government, I put up the Opaque Art projectors that hold the Federation Star in check."

PRIEST

"Oh…that's right, now I remeber you…you could have had a attractive and pleasing future! But then, you do this", shouting every word. Andrew and Gabriel were examining the episode, only those two know Nigel will be returning soon, with friends, allies. "You no longer have that career, you no longer have a homestead, you will join the meek and repulsive strain of unemployed rejects." The Priest pointed at two guards, came forward and struck David, thrashed him to the floor, beat him horribly. "People, our computers have given you pleasing music to listen to", he walked toward the center of the chamber, screaming to that everyone can hear, "We have given you our art, satisfying and pleasurable artifacts to keep your mind at rest. All the gifts of life! People....you have no need for ancient ways... our world is doing fine."

DAVID

In a fetal position on the floor, being smacked and abandoned by society, "But....individual freedoms...would open people's minds."

PRIEST

"No, no, no....quiet in conscious, calm in our right, confident our way is best!!" The Priest took several more steps to the center of the chamber, "We have taken care of everything, the people are taken care of...never need to wonder how or why! Everthing they need can and will be given to them by our way and computers!" He walked back over to David, beaten and still laying on the floor, pointed at him, "Just think about the average, what use have they for you? Forget about your silly whims, it does not fit the plan." The Priest walked over to Andrew and Gabriel, squinted eyes, whispered, "You two should think very carefully about your future...I do not like what I see." Turned around and screamed, "We are the Priests of the Temples of Syrinx, we control all!" Pointed to the guards, who took David to an exit, being homeless. Andrew and Gabriel looked at each other, knew Nigel will be here soon.

Sixth Chapter

David was taken to the sidewalk outside of the Priests cells and structure, the key for his jet was with his home key and was broken in half, he could see across the straight way, the terrace he was parked in, his jet was being confiscated by guards and security officers. Was it satisfactory that I held my ground? That I would rather stand by what I believe in rather than being submissive, a mere puppet kneeling below the Priests? He was a confused man watching his life being turned 180% in the other direction. I would have had a tolerable existance, everything I would need but have to remain intolereance to choices I would make as a free man? Submission? No! I could go to a different Galaxy, but with the Priests against me would not allow it, it would take a ton of currency. The other side of the planet? Unlikely, if I did they would send a missionary, a killer. "I need a drink", he whipered.

He walked alone, looked up at the beautiful structures and fabrications, the Priests have built a very amazing city, the metals and glass and pieces of construction are gorgeous, looked up at the Solar Federation Star, the design he fabricated was 8 miles across. The Baltan sea was 5 miles across between the east and west, a bridge between the east and west had a municipality floating in the water, connected to the bridge. The Star could be seen from space, glowing red, the Opaque art lets red only come out, a massive circle with a star within it, you could fly right through it and not feel a thing. The colassal edifices, one on the east and one on the west were almost 6 miles high, at the top of each one held the cells which made the star. David's job was to make sure it shines, that's it.

He finally found a Bistro where he ordered a whiskey and coke, "And keep them coming", he said to the waitress.

He sat and looked inside his mind, his thoughts about this afternoons actions. No matter which what I could turn the events, I absolutely cannot take submission! A good life, yes, good benefits from the inline government, yes, everything I need, yes, but analyzing and restricting and controlling that which pleases me, No! Leave this place, hard to do, another continent or simply leave this planet, again hard to do, the Priests would know.

Several hours later he needed sleep, across the pavement there was a boarding house, jets were flying by, by law they had to be above 20 feet above the ground so people on the street could walk, from 20 to 1000 feet jets were going in alignment, across the bridge and buildings. It was night and the city blazing, the gorgeous epitaphs were lit up and Megadon could be seen from space, a bright light with a Red Star of the Solar Ferderation on top, just what the Priests wanted.

"Hi", David said to the clerk, she was well dressed with a wided smile on her face, "What kind of room all you looking for sir, balcony, quiet room?"

"I will take a quiet room, I don't care where it is at", responded David. "I have a soundless room...", scanning on her computer, "on the 64th floor, looking out on the terrace." A soundless room keeps irratating noise from entering your suite, you can make the light as low as you want.

"I will take it, for just one night."

The elevator was almost silent and quick, off on 64 level and into his suite. Nice bed, a small couch pointed at a video screen and the window was as big as the wall it was on, he leaned against it and observed jets wissing by, the city was bright and was loominating with action, across the terrace he could see people in other buildings enjoying the night life. "I have got to think", he whispered to himself. Looked for another minute and went over to the bed table and hit the button "CLOSED". A pitch black covering went over the window, he hit "RELAXING SOUND", it sounded like a larger fan. He desparately laid back on the bed, 10 seconds ago you would not be able to you were downtown, it felt oh so good.

Several miles away, Gabriel and Andrew were scanning their telescope screen. Looking at the stars they could view a mini light 1000 light years away, they looked at each other.

GABRIEL

"Nigel will be back soon…with allies…much allies…..soon."

SEVENTH

Chapter

Director's note: Gabriel is Geddy Lee, Andrew is Alex Lifeson, Nigel is Neal Peart, Neal is also "The Oracle" that is in David's dream.

It took no time for David to fall asleep, good sleep cannot be overrated. The alcoholic beverages made the sleep come easy but did not slow his dreams and visions. He fell asleep rationalizing and reasoning his actions for the day, playing for the Priests, hoping they would find my concert appealing and help change their minds. It was too late for him to make them see a different way, their way is solid and will not be altered. The guitar was in his mind but the feeling of being a puppet for the Priests was intolerable, no submission.

He started thinking of the past, how man rose from beasts to modern man, to make life better than before. Man's creation and evolution to make vehicles and cities and the arts, individual freedom to escape from the ordinary and make something extraordinary.

His visions seemed so real, the horizon felt genuine, bona fide as he went from valleys to mountain tops. He rose with the clouds seeming like he was moving a thousand miles an hour yet like he was floating. At the top of a mountain he levitated, looked around at the planet below him. Thousands of feet down were the tops of clouds, valleys and other mountain tops easily visible.

He looked all around him, everything looked frozen but he felt nothing. A cloud in front of him was rising on the side of the mountain to him. As it risen, a man appeared standing on top of it, he stood there beyond a field of dreams, so real, so unique. As he got closer, David could see the smile on his face, he had long dark hair and a wide mustache and wore a grey robe. (Neil Peart, it is a dream, can easily use any film, then corroberated.)

ORACLE

"David, let us proceed to see what humans truly are."

As he raised his hands, we both accelerated to light speed and then some, the planet below me disappeared his vision, through galactic days and cosmic nights we raced through the entire galaxies, David could see how man rose from the beasts to create tribes, to communities, then to cities. David saw the works of gifted hands, create visions to reality.

Humans advance themselves forward, from cities and vehicles but also to the arts! Conceptual visions became reality, writings, music, paintings, sculptures, architecture, drawings and to even the abstract! They went from planet to planet where humans were showing their creativity.

ORACLE

"David, as humans rise, they have open eyes with the best for all in mind. The coverage of culture, history and moral values were in thought as man made cities and metropolises, from towns to megacities, we hold these truths to be self evident, for all societies and individuals. Their power grows with purpose strong to claim the home where they belong."

DAVID

"I....try to hold my individual rights in check."

ORACLE

"Yes David, I know...you love the guitar, playing it gives you freedom, gives you happiness. Your rights have been viled by the Priests, by neglecting your freedom, your dignity and justice have been completely rejected. You cannot let them take your spirit."

DAVID

"I...do not know...what to do."

ORACLE

"In time, you will know."

DAVID

"This...scene, seems so real, no intermediate at all...this vision...who are you...an Oracle?"

ORACLE

"Yes, I am an oracle, an inspiration to what humans can become. Do not let the Priests take away your imagination, they will tell you do not need to wonder how or why, we will take care of that for you! When you lose your open mind, your imagination and your creativity, you lose your spirit, you will become nothing but a toy to them, they call themselves the Priests but they are more government than spiritual, they have no care for your soul, they want to control your physical bodies."

DAVID

"I agree with you completely."

They saw many human colonies from the heavens, David could not tell if they were moving or it was just another scene, he felt half awake and aware and in a dream prod. When he looked up there were a million stars, far enough away yet close enough to see individual galaxies. This was a very wide dream state, to see man arising and to see the stars he was reaching for! The oracle was beyond mathematical equations, he has the dream within him all man are seeking.

ORACLE

"Remember David, you made a good humanistic decision in holding your dignity with the Priests, most of the people have bowed before the Priests, they need a leader, you cannot fight the Priests government, but you can send a message...remember David, send a message..."

The stars were flashing by, leaving beams of light through David's eyes, faster and faster, everything was turning white as he quickly regained consciousness.

DAVID

"Send a message."

EIGHTH Chapter

David sat on his bed and looked through his cell, he went to bed late and it was already mid-afternoon, remembering the dream. It seemed so real, the oracle told him to send a message, it took very little time to think of the action that needs to be done. He put his robe on and left the boarding house. He went across the roadway where jets were parked, he would have to rent one, he had to pay extra money to the officer because the Priests had put a bounty on any trading that David would do. Having that bounty on your head makes living extremely difficult. He quicky headed off to Grace to Glory, where he used to work, he thought, "I will have to break in, people will notice me, I will be an intruder after the Priests put a bounty on me."

He knew the building, he parked the jet about 500 yards away and walked up to the west side. There were windows below the see threw glass fence and if you were not seen, you could slice the glass and go in. He looked up at the Federation Star, he was right below it, the Grace to Glory building was made for to keep it shining for a thousand years, he gazed across the Baltan sea on both sides of the building, it was an amazing scene. Grace to Glory was floating, connected to the bridge across the edifices, contructed on the east and west sides of the Baltan sea, the Opaque Art Projectors were on top of the edifices, holding the Federation Star in sinc. The Star was eight miles wide, "Send a message."

It was quite easy getting in, he put on his hood from his robe, did his best not to be seen. Made his way to his old office, it was locked of course. Peered across the hall, no one was there, kneed the door hard, had to do it three times before the door opened, went inside put a chair against the door so it kept closed. He was very lucky his computer was still connected and in tact. It took him half an hour to complete his work. When he was done he put the chip in his pocket, he knew he would have to go to the main computer right below the star to finish his work, that was the only computer which held the Federation Star in alignment, same place where he put up the Star six months ago in front of the Priests, outside on the platform. He quickly remembered the celebration, putting the Star so everyone can see, the people and Priests applauding as the Star went up.

He went to the last hallway where he saw the door which lead to the main computer that kept the Star in alignment, it was outdoors on the platform, it was beneath steel and glass but the computer board was right in front of it, about 100 yards away when he got out the door. He heard a noise behind him...

He saw a worker deeming at him, pointing his finger at him and saw the same guard who beat him the other day focusing, judging him.

GUARD

"Stop right there intruder", he screamed out loud, "I will not harm you if you obey."

David swiftly opened the door, ran as fast as he could toward the Star computer, thought I will need a few seconds to put in the new site. He was almost at the site when he heard the door opened, he knew he had only seconds before the guard would be on top of him. He used all the speed he could to enter the new chip, looked behind, the guard was getting out his weapon as he was closing in on him. He was done, stared at the enter button and smiled, a thousand ideas, conceptions, convictions and reasoning went to his beliefs, the oracle said I would know what to do and he was right. This will send a message to all who can see. He hit the enter button, and took a step back, gazed up toward the Star, the guard shot him twice in the back, he went down on his knees and raised his arms, a beautiful smile on his face.

PRIEST

A few miles away, the higher Priests were having supper, went alarmed as what they saw in front of them, threw the glass they could see it rising, "What the......."

The people of Megadon could see it rise as well, a million of them could see it rising, a half smile on their face as they stood stunned.

Gabriel and Andrew stared at each other for a second, and smiled.

GABRIEL

"Good job David."

In front of the Federation Star, a man arose, naked in front of the star he held his arms out in front of the Federation Star, individual freedom versus government. The man stood against oppression, towards dignity, equality and justice. Eight miles high, he stood against the beliefs of the Priests, and everything for the Oracle and David witnessed in his dream!

THE FINAL

Chapter

PRIEST

The Priest was enraged, sitting with other Priests in an attractive cafe diner, he stood up with malice and hatred in his squinted eyes. "It is that... David..that rebel. I should have had him executed on site", he responded. "General", the upper Priests had a general and security guards in their presence continually, "Have a team remove that...mockery immediately!"

GENERAL

"Yes sir." He pulled out his cell to send orders. There was a beauty to the scene, the naked man in front of the Federation Star, long hair, his left arm was up higher than his right, was making a statement about oppression, take from me everything I own but still my spirit is much alive.

Gabriel and Andrew gazed at the the pleasing scene, red was the star, white was the man, it pushed back administative and executive orders from the Priests, it was directorate and clear, your governmental orders will not stand. The sun was going down, Andrew noticed that compact slices of light started appearing on the northeast sky.

ANDREW

"Ha ha...Nigel and our allies are arriving...perfect timing."

GENERAL

Back to the Priests, their General walked quickly to them and said, "Sir, there are ships coming out of hyper space...they are attack ships... hundreds of them."

PRIEST

"Are we in danger", his mouth wide open, nervousness was starting to fill him.

GENERAL

He looked out the widow, "Yes, I believe you are, I have had our defenses go to their ships, they should be out in half a minute, I have also have your ship ready to go, if need

PRIEST

"To hell with that...we are going now...other Priests come." All 15 of them followed the executive Priest.

DAVID

Back to David, still on his knees, looking at the man against the Federation Star, the guard had his weopon pointed at David but his mouth wide open in awe, saw the ghost like man standing miles in height in front of the star, saw the attack ships coming out of hyper space, he did not know what to do. David smile was ear to ear, it was all in front of him, the scene of taking out oppression was right in front of him, he fell, his life was coming to an end.

The people of Megadon were in awe, the sun was going down over the horizon, the Opaque projectors had the Star held high, now a naked man stood 8 miles high in front of it. Citizens could see the white flahes of attack ships coming out of hyper space, hundreds of them. They started taking positions in attack formations, flying by so fast, long thin missiles were launched causing massive explosions at the base of the edifices, the structures trembled but held their ground. The bottom of the east structure is where defense ships came out, to defend what the Priests made for Megadon, hundreds of them, to defend what Priests held true. The star and the man were seen from the light spectrum, the ships could fly right through them. Hundreds of ships to defend the Priests versus the Old Republic allied ships! The citizens watched in amazement, they were astonished at what they saw.

GABRIEL

"They are from Andromeda, near the M31 area, always have been our friends, if they beat the Priests cruise ships, freedom will be returned to this planet", said Gabriel, Andrew agreed with him and watched the fire fight.

500 allied ships vs 500 Priest ships, fighting inside a Federation Star and a man holding his hands against oppression! Jets inside the Magadon were flying away from the fight. Thousands of people were quickly getting out of harms way, on their jets or quickly running.

Citizens more than 5 miles away on east and west sides of the Baltan sea were astonished and enjoyed watching the fray, every couple of seconds a ship would detonate, explode when it took a missile or an emission liquid laser. The allied ships knew that to defeat their oppression enemies, that Megadon would also free the entire planet, who ever has Megadon controls the entire planet.

PRIEST

Yelling out loud, "Is my ship ready to go", they were almost toward the east edifice where the Priests vessel was kept.

GENERAL

"Yes, it just finished powering up."

Priest

"We will go into orbit, watch the fight, after we defeat them, punish those necessary for this...interruption!" The General had a bizarre look on his face, the Priest saw it, "We will defeat them, won't we?"

General

He looked at his cell, "My information tells me when one of our ships is...destroyed or dismantled...it will no longer send out a signal...we are... losing." The Priest swiftly felt very humiliated, eyes wide open.

The pilots of the allies and the Priests were conflicted, they flew threw the air and threw the Star and man, as they piloted their single man ships they saw everything was a bit more red threw the Star and a bit more white threw the man. They hoped to level, to destroy the ship in front of them hoping there was no ship behind them ready to do the same. Their ships move so fast yet turn so quickly and gracefully. More missiles were racking into the base of the edifices, massive explosions but still the still stood up, you could feel the trembling as the detonation massed the structure. At the outer end of the east edifice the Priests ship was coming out.

Priest

"Get my ship into orbit!"

General

"Not all of the Priests are here, it will only be a couple seconds before...."

Priest

Screaming, "Take off now, that's an order!" The general followed the order, the sizeable vessel closed doors and the massive ship flyed through the hollow large deck until it was out in open space. The pilots and the Priests could see massive explosions at the base of the edifices and above them lightening explosions of fighter ships were detonated by its enemy.

The Star and the Man held their ground, held in position as the fray continued. "General, have our ship go into hyper space, go to the closest Federation system available!"

GENERAL

"Yes sir."

It was too late, out of his peripheral vision the Priest saw a curve of single pilot fighter ships coming their way through his window, he looked. Ten...a dozen of fighter ships coming right at them, he whispered to himself, tried to keep his faith. "I am a Priest...the lesser man should be on his knees before me", now yelling, stood up, "I am a Priest...through the Federation, the Priests of the Temples of Syrinx have control of this system", he looked back through his window at the enemy ships, each of the dozen ships launched two missiles, 24 missiles coming right at his ship. He knew he had seconds to live but still kept his faith, "The Federation will always rule...all systems, I mean all will bow in front...", the missiles hit. The core of the engines of the ship were nuclear, the explosion was massive, it was like the sun rising in the distance. The light of the Star and Man became unseeable as the fire ball could be seen from outer space.

GABRIEL

"That had to be the Priests vessel", Gabriel said to Andrew, "From the looks of it, the Priests are losing...but all that means is they will find another system to conquer."

ANDREW

"That's all right, this system is now free!"

As the fray was coming to an end, explosions could still be seen as fighter ships would still annihilate. Gabriel and Andrew could see a small ship arriving at their small port right outside their homes. It quickly landed and doors were opened on it's port side.

GABRIEL

"Good evening, Nigel."

NIGEL

"Good evening brothers", he said as he walked toward them, he still had a helmit on his head. "How was the last 6 months, I came back as soon as I could, had to make sure we had enough fire power to defeat our foe...the Priests."

ANDREW

"Yes, we understand that", they all looked toward the sky, a lightening streak of white light came in view as a considerable size craft came out of hyper space above the Federation star. Detonations at the base of the edifices made the ground tremble, the Opaque projectors were losing power, the Star was fading, only the Man stood in front of Megadon! The cruise ship was from M31, it lead out a message to the planet and surrounding sytems.

"ATTENTION ALL PLANETS OF SOLAR FEDERATION--ATTENTION ALL PLANETS OF THE SOLAR FEDERATION--ATTENTION ALL PLANETS OF THE SOLAR FEDERATION---WE HAVE ASSUMED CONTROL--WE HAVE ASSUMED CONTROL--WE HAVE ASSUMED CONTROL"

NIGEL

"It had to be done."

GABRIEL

"Nigel, let me show you what Andrew and I were doing the last 6 months", they walked into Gabriels place, as the fight was coming to an end, occasional explosion of a ship could be heard, Nigel removes his helmet.

(It was Geddy, Alex and Neil)

They went in Gabriels place, he took out a remote and opened up two huge 40 foot granite marbels, hidden from outward eyes of the Priests, as they opened across the floor there was a place where Andrew was making his own guitars, next to it, Gabriel was building a wooden 22 fret acoustic bass. Between the pillars there were places to write, scrolls, a place for pictures, drawings and sculptures. Toward the very end of it was an oil painting, it was mostly done, it was David, when Gabriel and Andrew enjoyed watching him play the guitar he found inside the cave by the Baltan sea, through memory they put him down on canvas. He was smiling as he played his beautiful guitar, sitting on the rock next to the cave.

NIGEL

"Did you know him?"

GABRIEL

"Yes", as they looked at the painting, "He loved the arts and true nature of man."

NIGEL

"This may sound strange...but I can almost remember him...from a dream."

ANDREW

"The design is almost...flawless. Gifted hands and open minds, anything is possible."

They look at the painting and turn back to the 2112, Geddy, Alex and Neil looking at the painting. They go back again to the 2112, the movie starts with this 2112 photo and ends with it.

NEIL PEART

1952 to 2020

Neil Peart, the virtuoso drummer and lyricist of the Rock Progressive Band Rush. I could enter dozens of his awards and books and trialers of his past but you could see that on any memoirs written about his past, I will put in what he meant to me. Truthfully, I am crying as I write this. My family is number 1, other than that, Neil was a massive portion of what I am. I always wanted to write from high school years, knowing and remembering his lyrics made me write. I am that guy who knows every lyric written by Neil, some people say I am a nerd, that's crap. If you know what the reasons and intelligence behind his words, you are not a nerd, you just simply know better, the music means more. I saw them play live 14 times, for true fans, that's nothing. One thing I know that is true is once you are a fan you will always be one. The one thing about Rush is that they have several positives going in their favor, the lyrics, Alex's solos, Geddy's bass style while he sings and moves his microphone with his nose! It never ends! Neil's drum solos! Oh please stop!

Like 10 million people, I have listened to 2112 a thousand times. I did not have to think about how a movie should be done too long, David's naked man telling the Federation Star it was no longer welcome was easy.

I just had to have him put it up at the same time the allies were taking the Priests war machine. I like to think that my writing makes me feel like Neil when he wrote, writing is the most pleasurable thing I had ever done. The last thing I would like to say is that I know what suffering is, Neil did too. I have 2 children with autism, Neil lost his entire family. You try your best to deal with it every day.

9 781958 122440